VIKING KESTREL

Viking Penguin Inc., 40 West 23rd Street
New York, New York 10010, U.S.A.
Penguin Books Canada Limited, 2801 John Street
Markham, Ontario, Canada L3R 1B4
Text copyright © Karen Erickson, 1987
Illustrations copyright © Maureen Roffey, 1987
All rights reserved
First published in 1987 by Viking Penguin Inc.
Published simultaneously in Canada
Set in Sabon.
Printed in Italy by L.E.G.O.
Produced for the publishers by
Sadie Fields Productions Ltd, London.

1   2   3   4   5   91   90   89   88   87

I Was So Mad

Karen Erickson and Maureen Roffey

Viking Kestrel

Nobody will play with me.
Nobody will listen to me.

Everybody teases me.
Everyone is mean.

I'm really mad.

I want to hit and kick and punch
someone – maybe my sister.

I want to shout mean things.

I want to break something.

But Mommy says I can't. It isn't fair.

She says I can hit my pillow or
punch my bed.

I can make ugly, angry faces in
the mirror.

I can go outside and kick a ball, stomp
around, and shout at the sky.

Everybody feels angry sometimes.

I can get mad without hurting anybody
or breaking anything.
I can do it.
I did it.